Oliver Optic, Oliver Optic

The Christmas Gift

A Story for Little Folks

Oliver Optic, Oliver Optic

The Christmas Gift
A Story for Little Folks

ISBN/EAN: 9783743427464

Manufactured in Europe, USA, Canada, Australia, Japa

Cover: Foto ©Andreas Hilbeck / pixelio.de

Manufactured and distributed by brebook publishing software
(www.brebook.com)

Oliver Optic, Oliver Optic

The Christmas Gift

In the Play Room.

RIVERDALE STORY BOOKS

THE CHRISTMAS GIFT

JOHN ANDREW

BOSTON, LEE & SHEPARD.

The Riverdale Books.

THE CHRISTMAS GIFT.

A STORY FOR LITTLE FOLKS.

BY

OLIVER OPTIC,

AUTHOR OF "THE BOAT CLUB," "ALL ABOARD," "NOW OR NEVER," "TRY
AGAIN," "POOR AND PROUD," "LITTLE BY LITTLE," &c.

BOSTON:
LEE AND SHEPARD,
(SUCCESSORS TO PHILLIPS, SAMPSON & CO.)
1870.

ELECTROTYPED AT THE
BOSTON STEREOTYPE FOUNDRY.

THE CHRISTMAS GIFT.

I.

THERE were to be great times at Mr. Lee's house during the Christmas Holidays. Frank and Flora had long looked forward to this season, for they expected to enjoy themselves more than ever before.

(7)

Their two cousins, Henry and Sarah Vernon, were to spend a week with them; and this alone would have made them very happy. Besides this, Christmas was to be celebrated in a manner worthy of the occasion.

The windows of the parlor and sitting room had been dressed with evergreen, and looked very pretty. And the day before Christmas, when

Flora wanted to enter the parlor, she found the doors were all locked. At first she did not know what to make of this, for she had never known the doors to be fastened before.

She was going to ask her mother why the doors were locked, when she happened to think that her father and mother might want to surprise the children in some

manner, and she decided not
to say any thing about the
matter.

Henry and Sarah came in
the noon train, and their
cousins were very glad to see
them. They lived in the city,
and had a great deal to say
about the fine things at home.
Then Frank had to tell about
his voyage down the river on
a raft. The city cousins felt a
deep interest in this story, for

they had heard their parents speak of it.

Flora had no story to tell, and seemed to be thrown into the shade by the fine talk of her city cousins, and the great doings of her brother Frank. But she was thinking of something all the time — something that was a great deal better than fine talk, or even sailing on the river.

She had a great plan in her

head.   She had been thinking of it for two or three weeks. Indeed, she had been so kind of sober while she thought, that her parents feared she might be sick.   She was almost always laughing, and was as fond of play as any little girl you ever saw.

It is no wonder, therefore, that her father and mother thought she must be sick, for this plan had made a great change in her, — just as when boys and girls become men and women, and have a great many things to think about, they have to stop playing, and do not laugh half so much as when they were children.

After dinner, the children all met in the play room. It was a nice little chamber up stairs, where Frank and Flora kept their playthings, and where they played in stormy weather. I dare say all my little readers would have enjoyed a visit to this room, for it was a perfect museum of playthings.

In one corner there was a complete doll's house. It is true, there was but one room in Miss Dolly's mansion, but it had ever so many fine things in it.

It was about a yard square. Two sides of the room were

formed of the two sides of
the chamber, while the other
two were made of a kind of
fence, about six inches high.

This little chamber had a
carpet of its own — and a
very pretty carpet it was, too.
I believe it was a piece of
drab cashmere, with a handsome figure on it; and it
looked just like a carpet.

In one corner stood the
bed. It was nicely made up,

with a clean white spread, and real sheets and pillows. The bedstead was made of rosewood, and the corners were carved; and if you had seen it, you would have said it was the prettiest one in the world.

There was a centre table in the middle of the room, on which were placed two or three of the tiniest books you ever saw. One of them was

called "A Picture of London."
It was given to Flora by her
friend Mr. Bigelow, a book-
seller in the city. Another
was "The Life of Tom Thumb."
Neither of these books was
more than an inch square;
and they were just big enough
for the little centre table.

Six tiny chairs stood around
the room, besides two sofas,
and a rocking chair. Near
the bed was a handsome

stuffed arm-chair, in which Miss Dolly herself was seated.

Miss Dolly was a very pretty young lady. She had a wax head, with glass eyes, and real hair. She was clothed in a white muslin dress, trimmed with satin ribbon. It was rather a cool dress for Christmas; but I suppose Flora thought she ought to look like a bride at this time, though it was winter.

Her cousin Sarah had never seen Miss Dolly or her mansion house before, and she was so pleased that she danced with delight. She had to take up Miss Dolly herself, and examine every article of her dress. Then she picked up every article in the room and looked at it. Not content with this, the bed had to be pulled to pieces, and re-made, so that she could see every part of it.

Henry Vernon, being a boy, was, of course, *above* taking an interest in dollies and baby-houses. But he could not help being pleased with the pretty room in which Miss Dolly lived. He looked at the bed, the sofas, and the chairs, and said some smart things about dolls and baby-houses in general.

He then turned his atten-
tion to the rocking-horse, the
tin steamboat, and other won-
derful things that were in the
play room.   Frank showed
him all the toys, hoops, rattles,
and "things" he had.   By the
time he had finished, and the
girls had put Miss Dolly's
room to rights, Flora called
the meeting to order by hint-
ing that she had something
to say.

All were ready to hear her; but poor Flora was so wild over her great plan, that she could hardly say what she wished. She had been thinking of something for a long time, and she almost trembled for fear the others would not like her plan.

"Do you know what I have been thinking about these three weeks?" said she, her pretty face red with excitement.

"How should we know?" replied Henry, with a laugh.

"Was it about a sleigh ride?" asked Sarah.

"No; nothing of that kind."

"A Christmas tree?"

"No; guess again."

"About having a party?"

"No."

"What was it?"

"When you guess right, I'll tell you."

"Wasn't it about a rag

baby?" said Henry, with a sneer.

"No, it wasn't."

They all guessed round several times, but none of them guessed right. By this time Flora was calm enough to unfold her great plan.

"Do you know there is a poor woman in Riverdale—"

"Lots of them," put in Henry.

"But there is one poor wo-

man in Riverdale that I want
to tell you about. She is a
widow — that means that she
hasn't got any body to take
care of her."

Henry burst out in a hearty
laugh, which quite surprised
poor Flora; and she wondered
what she had said that was so
funny.

"Do you suppose we don't
know what a widow is?" asked
Henry, who was a city boy,

and rather smart. " Besides, a widow isn't a woman that hasn't got any one to take care of her."

"No one but David, I mean," added Flora, who felt that she had made a mistake.

" Who is David ? " said Sarah.

"He is the poor widow's son; and he is a real nice boy. He sells newspapers and gets money for his poor mother; and she thinks there is not another boy like David in the world."

"Does she, indeed! What a funny mother she must be, to be sure!" laughed Henry.

"Hush!" said Flora; "there comes my mother, and I don't want her to know any thing about it yet."

So they all went to playing with Dolly and the rocking-horse; but Mrs. Lee did not

stop but a moment. She only
came in to see what the children were about; for they
laughed so loud, she was
afraid they were doing some
mischief.

COUNTING THE MONEY.

II.

JUST as soon as Mrs. Lee had left the room, the little party gathered round Flora again to find out what she had been thinking about. They all wanted to know. Even Henry, who talked so big, and felt so big, was just as eager as Sarah and Frank.

"David White — that's the

poor widow's son — earns lots of money by selling papers. But his mother is very poor," continued Flora.

"You told us that before," said Henry.

"Dear me! so I did.   Well — his mother is very poor."

"That's three times you have said it."

"What ails me?" laughed Flora. "I believe I can't say what I wanted."

"Try again, then," added Sarah.

"Well, Mrs. White — that's the poor widow's name — as she is very poor —— "

The children all laughed then till their sides ached, and Master Henry had nearly smashed Miss Dolly's quarters all to pieces, he was so much amused because Flora said the same thing so many times.

"Never mind him," said Sarah. "Now go on, Flora."

"Well, I was just going to say that Mrs. White was very poor ——"

"You *did* say that," roared Henry; and they all laughed again till they were as red as red apples.

"I declare — well then — but people say they don't see how poor Mrs. White will be able to get through the winter. They say the times are very hard, and that she can't get any work."

" But where is that smart son of hers ? "

"O, he earns lots of money; but then the poor folks don't buy so many papers in hard times. He has got lots of brothers and sisters."

" How many ? — about two hundred ? " asked Henry.

"Dear me ! Of *course* not,"

replied Flora, with a twist of
the head that made that heap
of pretty curls fly all over her
rosy cheeks. " He has got
two brothers, and two sisters,
besides himself."

" Is he his own brother ? "
laughed Henry.

" Of course he isn't."

" You said he had two
brothers, and two sisters, *besides himself.*"

" Well, you city boys are so

very proper!" said Flora, with a pout of her cherry lips. "I mean that his mother has two boys and two girls besides David."

"O, then David is a girl," cried Henry.

"How particular you are!" said Flora, with another pout. "Won't you please to say it for me?"

"You mean that she has four children besides David."

"That is just what I mean," added Flora, who was pleased to have the matter settled. "She can't take care of them all this winter, and something must be done to help her."

"Isn't there an almshouse in Riverdale?" asked Henry.

"Why, she don't want to go to the almshouse. How would you like to go to the almshouse, Henry?"

"I shouldn't like it; but I am not a pauper."

"What's a pauper?" asked Flora.

"Why, a poor person that has to be taken care of by the town or city."

"You may be a pauper one of these days."

"I guess not."

"Would you like to be sent off to the almshouse, if you were?"

"I don't know but I should."

"Well, Mrs. White don't, any way. And I am going to do something to help her."

"You! what can you do?" sneered Henry.

"I have got lots of money. I have got a savings bank, and it is almost full. I am going to buy a lot of things to-night — a barrel of flour, some sugar, some tea, some coffee, some potatoes, and —

O, lots of things! I am going to get father to let me have a horse and wagon, and to-morrow morning we will all go over to Mrs. White's with the things."

"That will be first rate, Flora," said Frank. "She shall have all my money, too, and I've got more than you have."

"You are real good, Frank," replied Flora. "We can buy

ever so many things. Won't
we have a nice time! And
won't Mrs. White be glad, and
won't she be surprised when
we take the things in to her!"

"Won't she, though!"

"We must send her a load
of wood too. Don't you want
to give something, Henry?"

"Yes, I should like to, but
I haven't got much to give."

"I have got a dollar, and
so have you," said Sarah.

"I don't want to give all of it. I want to buy something for myself."

"I will give all of mine."

"I will give half a dollar," added Henry.

Then Frank and Flora took their money boxes out of a drawer in the play room. They were little wooden boxes with holes in the top to slip the money through. Each of them had a key, and the savings banks were emptied upon the floor.

Henry helped Flora count her money, and they found there was two dollars and seventy cents. Frank's box had contained three dollars and twenty cents. The two cousins gave a dollar and a half; and the whole sum for the poor widow was seven dollars and forty cents.

To the children this was a

great sum of money, and they thought it would pay all of Mrs. White's expenses for the winter. Frank was chosen to keep the funds, and he put them into one of the boxes. Then Flora said they had better go down and tell her father all about the plan, and he would show them how to go to work.

Flora was so delighted, she could not walk, but went

dancing down the stairs and through the entries. She kept thinking all the time how glad the poor widow would be to see the things, and how happy they would all be when they carried them to her.

Mr. and Mrs. Lee were in the sitting room when the party rushed through the entry. They saw that "something was in the wind," and Mr. Lee threw down the newspaper which the little merchant had just brought to him, and Mrs. Lee stopped sewing. The children came just as though the house was on fire, and they would all be burnt to death if they did not run as fast as ever they could.

"Father!" shouted Flora, as she bolted into the room, followed by the others.

"What is the matter, my dear? Have you hurt you?"

"O, no, father. I've got something to tell you — something first rate; and I want you to help me — I mean we — for we are all going to do it."

"What are you going to do? I should think you meant to set the river afire!"

"O, no, nothing of that kind, father.   We are going to give a Christmas present to Mrs. White.   You know she is very poor, and has a hard time to take care of all her family."

"She has, indeed, my child."

"We have put all our money together, and we are going to buy a load of wood, a barrel of flour, lots of potatoes, and meat, and coffee, and tea, sugar, and — and — pepper, and salt, and mustard —— "

"Stop, stop, my child! You will have a fit if you run on in this way."

Her father and mother, and
the children, all laughed to
hear Flora talk so fast, and
add such things as pepper
and mustard to her list. I
suppose they thought the poor
widow could get along very
well without such things as
these.

Mr. Lee said he liked the
plan, and that he would take
the money and buy such
things as he thought Mrs.

White needed. He promised to have every thing ready for them to start at eight o'clock the next morning.

While the children were at tea, the parlor doors were unlocked, and the room lighted. One end was occupied by a beautiful Christmas tree, which was covered all over with candles and pretty things.

When Flora and Frank and their cousins entered the par-

lor, they were very much surprised, for none of them had
ever seen any thing so brilliant
before, and they all passed a
merry Christmas Eve.

THE PROCESSION.

III.

THE children were up bright and early at Mr. Lee's on Christmas morning. They had expected a visit from Santa Claus during the night, and the stockings had all been left so that he could easily find them.

Truly Santa Claus had been kind to them, for the stockings

were not only well filled, but
a table was also covered all
over with fine things. There
were all kinds of playthings,
and books, and games, and
pictures.

The parents of Frank and
Flora were rich, and could
afford to give them a great
many nice things. I don't
think they cared so much for
playthings as some children
I have seen. They had so

many of them that they did
not value them as some poorer
children would have done.

After Flora had emptied
her stocking, and gathered
up the books, games, and pictures that belonged to her, she
told Frank she wished she had
all the money they cost, so
that she could give it to poor
Mrs. White.

Frank said he wished he
had the money for his pres-

ents, for he was sure it would make the poor widow happier than the things would him. But they were both very grateful to their parents for thinking of them, — for they knew that Santa Claus was only another name for father and mother.

All the little boys and girls don't know this. Emma — that is one of my little girls — asked me if I did not take out the register, so that Santa Claus could get into the room, and fill up her stocking.   But she is only four years old.

"Merry Christmas" rang through the house till break-fast was over, and then the children were in a great hurry to make the visit to Mrs. White.   Mr. Lee had gone out early in the morning, and they were all sure that he would do every thing right.

At eight o'clock, Mrs. Lee had bundled up the children in their warm hoods and cloaks, ready for a start. Then they wanted to be off at once, and Flora's mother could hardly keep her from running out in the cold, before the things were ready. ·

I suppose my readers all know that in the city, or any where, when they want to have a great time, they get up a procession, and march through the streets. They sometimes have wagons, and chariots, and carriages.

Mr. Lee, who was very glad to find that the children were so kind as to remember the poor widow on Christmas, meant to surprise them. So he got up a kind of procession. Perhaps you will think it was a queer procession; but it pleased the children ever so much, and Flora was almost wild with delight.

While they were looking out the window, they saw Mr. Lee drive up with the carryall. He came very slowly, for behind him was a wagon with a cord of wood on it, drawn by two yokes of oxen. Then came a cart with two barrels of potatoes, a barrel of flour, and a barrel of apples on it. Behind this was a wagon loaded with buckets of sugar, rice, coffee, with packages of tea, salt, and other groceries; a ham, a turkey, a keg of salt pork; and a great many other things.

Flora screamed with delight when she saw this procession. It was more grand than an army of soldiers, and she thought she would rather go in it than be the Queen of England.

Frank was pleased, and so were the two city cousins. Henry even went so far as to wish he had given all his money, instead of half of it.

The children all bolted out at the front door, and Mr. Lee helped them into the carryall.

"This is first rate, father," said Flora. "Won't Mrs. White be surprised!"

"I think she will be," replied Mr. Lee. "She will

have good reason to be surprised."

" I hope you have got lots
of things."

" I have."

" Did you spend all the
money ? "

" Yes; every cent of it, my
child."

" And more too," said Henry, as he looked back upon
the procession of " goodies."

" Did you, father ? "

5

"I thought I would add a little to your gift," said Mr. Lee, with a smile.

"How kind you are, father!"

"But all the things shall be called the children's Christmas gift."

Mr. Lee got into the carriage, and told the drivers of the wagons to follow him. The two horses were wide awake. They did not want to wait for the slow oxen, but Mr. Lee made them, for he wanted the procession to keep together.

When the procession had got about half way to Mrs. White's house, a man covered with dirt and rags stopped the carriage. He said he was very poor, and had not eaten any thing since the morning before.

"Poor man!" said Flora. "Do give him something, father."

"Bless you, little miss! Your father is too kind to refuse me," said the man.

"I can't do any thing for you," said Mr. Lee, firmly.

"Do, father," added Flora.

"Any small change, to buy me something to eat," said the man, in pleading tones.

"If you are hungry, go to my house, and my wife will feed you," replied Mr. Lee.

"Won't you give me the

matter of a few cents?"
begged the man.

"Not a cent."

"I will," said Henry. "I
don't want the poor man to
go hungry;" and he threw
him a ten-cent piece.   .

"God bless you, my little
man!" said the beggar, as he
picked up the money. "May
you never want for a meal of
victuals!"

Mr. Lee started his horses,

and the procession again moved on. Flora wondered that her father should deny the poor man. She pitied him very much, when he said he had eaten nothing since the morning before. She thought what a dreadful thing it was to be hungry, and have nothing to eat.

She wanted to cry, she felt so badly, and she thought her father was very hard not to give him a little money when he needed it so much. If she had only had some money, she would have given him the whole of it.

"You did very wrong, Henry," said Mr. Lee, when they had gone a little way farther.

"Wrong, sir?" replied Henry. "Why, didn't the man say he had eaten nothing for a whole day."

"That may be, and it may not be."

"But I know he was hungry by the looks of him," said Flora.

"Those who have any thing to give away ought to be very careful to whom they give it. The man looked like a drunk-ard. Very likely he will spend the money you gave him, Henry, for liquor. It is not charity to give a man rum."

"Do you think he is a bad man, father?" asked Flora.

"I don't know that he is. I told him to go to the house, and your mother would give him something to eat. You saw that he wanted money more than food. I am afraid, Henry, your money will do him more hurt than good."

"I hope not, uncle."

"It is not charity to give money to such persons. When

you have any thing to give,
you ought to use a great deal
of care.   We should visit the
poor, and find out about them."

"We know Mrs. White is
good," said Flora.

"We do; and we may give
to her without fear."

The children had learned a
new lesson about giving — a
lesson which every body ought
to learn.

THE CHRISTMAS TREE.

IV.

MRS. WHITE, the poor widow, had been able to get along very well while she could obtain work, and while David, her oldest son, could sell plenty of newspapers. But it was very hard times, and there was not much work to be done; so the poor had to get along as well as they could.

Many of the mills had ceased to work because the times were so hard, and therefore the men who had bought a paper every day could not afford to do so now. David lost about one half of his trade. His mother earned very little, and she had no idea how she should be able to get through the hard winter.

On that bright, cold Christmas morning, the poor widow

thought how happy the rich must be, who had plenty to eat, and plenty of coal to keep them warm. She thought of the future, and feared she should be obliged to ask the town to help her. She did not want to do this, but she could not think of letting her children suffer for the want of food, or shiver in the cold.

While she was thinking of these things, Mr. Lee drove

up to the front door, and the
children all got out of the
carryall.   Mrs. White wondered what they had come
for, and she was still more
surprised when she saw the
great load of wood, the cart
with the barrels, and the wagon
full of buckets and bundles.

She did not know what to
make of it, for she did not
understand that all these
things were for her,

"I wish you a merry Christmas!" shouted Flora, as she rushed into the kitchen, where Mrs. White and the children were.

"Thank you, Miss Flora," replied Mrs. White. "May you live to see a great many, and all of them happy as the present."

All the rest of the children wished the poor widow and all her family a merry Christmas. Flora capered about the room, almost beside herself with joy.

"We have brought you lots of good things, Mrs. White," said she, when the children had all wished the family a merry Christmas. "We put all our money together, and bought you a load of wood, some flour, and potatoes, and apples, and tea, and sugar, and pepper, and salt, and mustard, and —— "

"That will do, Flora," said her father. "Mrs. White will soon find out what you have brought."

"I am very grateful to you all, children, for thinking of me. May God reward you for your kindness!" replied Mrs. White, with tears in her eyes.

"We wanted to make it a happy day for you, and David, and the rest of the children," added Flora.

"It will be the happiest day I have seen for a month," said Mrs. White. "I was thinking this very morning what would become of us; but you have filled my home with plenty. I shall never forget you, children."

Then Flora danced three or four times round the room, for she was so happy she could not keep still. I hope my readers have all found out that " it is more blessed to give than to receive." I am sure Flora and Frank were quite as happy as the poor widow — though her fears about her children being cold and hungry had suddenly been driven away.

She felt that God had heard her prayers, and made these children the agents of his bounty. Her eyes were full of tears, but they were tears

of joy. As she heard the rat-
tling of the sticks of wood
which the men were throw-
ing from the wagon, it seemed
like sweet music to her ears.
Then the barrels were rolled
into the kitchen, the buckets
placed in the closet, and the
bundles on the table, so that
the room looked just as though
she had set up a store.

"These things are the Christmas gift of the children," said

Mr. Lee, when the articles had all been brought into the house. " They got up the affair themselves, without my knowledge. No one told them to do it; and I am sure they will all remember to-day as one of the happiest days of their lives."

" They are very kind ; and I shall think of them and pray for them as long as I live," replied Mrs. White. " I

was afraid this morning that
we should all have to go to
the poorhouse. I spoke to
David about it, and the poor
boy cried as though his heart
would break. He is a very
tender-hearted child."

"I hope I shall be able to
pay you for all these things
some time," said David.

"O, we don't want any pay,"
exclaimed Flora. "That would
spoil every thing. This is our

Christmas gift, David. You wouldn't pay for a gift — would you, David?"

"You are very good, and I hope I shall be able to do something for you one of these days, Flora," replied David. "You are very rich, and we are very poor, so that we can't do much for you."

"Yes, you can," said Flora.

"What can I do?"

"You can love us; and

that is all we want — isn't it, father ? "

. " Yes, my child ; and we must always deserve their love. We may yet be poor, and David may yet be very rich."

" When he is, David will be good to us, I know. Wouldn't it be funny, if we should get poor, and David should bring us a load of wood, some potatoes, flour, tea, sugar, and apples ? "

"And mustard and pepper," added Henry, laughing.

"It would not be very funny for us, but I know we should be thankful to him," replied Mr. Lee, with a smile.

"Well, David, when things change, you shall do for us what we have done for you, and then it will be all square."

"I hope you never will be poor, but if you are, I will give you every thing I have," said

David, in a feeling and earnest tone.

The children stopped nearly an hour at the little black cottage; but they were so happy, it seemed like a palace to them. They had all felt the luxury of doing good. The plenty they had carried to the home of the poor family filled their own hearts with plenty—with love and peace.

Before they went away, Mr.

Lee gave Mrs. White money
enough to buy some warm
clothes for all the children, and
for herself. She had nothing
more to fear from the cold
winter and hard times; and
she hoped in the spring to be
able to take care of her family
herself.

The party, so happy they
could hardly keep from shout-
ing, bade the family good by,
and started for home. As they

passed through the village, they saw, in front of a store where rum was sold, two men fighting. They were soon parted by some people, and Henry saw that one of them was the man to whom he had given the money.

Mr. Lee said he had been drinking. He stopped the horses, and asked a gentleman who the man was. He was told that he was a poor man

who spent all he could earn
for liquor, and that he had
just taken enough to make
him ugly, so that he wanted
to fight.

"You see what good your
money has done, Henry," said
Mr. Lee, as he started the
horses.

"Yes, sir; it has done more
harm than good.   I will never
give money again, unless I am
pretty sure that it will do good."

"That is a good lesson for you to learn. It is not charity to give to every one that asks us."

In a little while the party reached Mr. Lee's house, where they had a nice time all the rest of the day — a better time, I am sure, for having begun the day with a good deed.